KT-155-614

What's Going On, Gus?

by

Jill Atkins

Illustrated by Kate Aldous

For Dave, the perfect model
for Gus's Dad!

First published in Great Britain by Barrington Stoke Ltd
10 Belford Terrace, Edinburgh, EH4 3DQ
Copyright © 1999 Jill Atkins
Illustrations © Kate Aldous
The moral right of the author has been asserted in
accordance with the Copyright, Designs and
Patents Act 1988
ISBN 1-902260-10-4

Printed by BPC-AUP (Aberdeen) Ltd, Aberdeen
The publisher acknowledges subsidy from the Scottish Arts Council
towards the publication of this volume

THE SCOTTISH ARTS COUNCIL

Meet The Author - Jill Atkins

What is your favourite animal?
A cat
What is your favourite boy's name?
Benjamin
What is your favourite girl's name?
Rebecca
What is your favourite food?
Pizza
What is your favourite music?
Classical
What is your favourite hobby?
Walking

Meet The Illustrator - Kate Aldous

What is your favourite animal?
A cat
What is your favourite boy's name?
Daniel
What is your favourite girl's name?
Alice
What is your favourite food?
Curry
What is your favourite music?
Classical
What is your favourite hobby?
Playing the piano

Barrington Stoke was a famous and much loved story-teller. He travelled from village to village, carrying a lantern to light his way. He arrived as it grew dark and when the young boys and girls of the village saw the glow of his lantern, they hurried to the central meeting place. They were full of excitement and expectation, for his stories were always wonderful.

Then Barrington Stoke set down his lantern. In the flickering light the listeners were enthralled by his tales of adventure, horror and mystery. He knew exactly what they liked best and he loved telling a good story. And another. And then another. When the lantern burned low and dawn was nearly breaking, he slipped away. He was gone by morning, only to appear the next day in some other village to tell the next story.

Contents

Chapter 1
The Babysitter

"Gus," said Mum, "You *will* be sensible while we're out, won't you?"

I was sitting at the dining-room table. I looked up from my chemistry experiment and nodded.

"When am I anything else?" I said with a grin.

Mum hopped past me, almost ready but missing one shoe. She almost bumped into Dad.

1

He was standing in front of the mirror in the
hall, picking gravy stains off his sweatshirt
and bits of gunge out of his beard.

"Anyone seen my other shoe?" Mum asked.

"S'oo," boomed a voice from the other side of
the room. It was Boomer. He was on his potty.

"Boomer's got it," I said.

Mum pulled the shoe from Boomer's mouth.

"Look at it!" she said crossly. "All soggy."

"Soggy s'oo!" said Boomer. "Soggy s'oo!"

Mum put on her shoe and turned to Dad.

"Hurry up!" she said. "We'll be late."

"*I'm* ready," said Dad, "but where's the babysitter?"

I hate the word babysitter. I'm no baby! I was just about to complain about it when there was a ring at the front door.

"Ah!" said Dad and he hurried to let her in.

"Who's babysitting?" asked my sister, Yeti.

She was sitting at the opposite end of the dining-room table from me, eating syrup sandwiches. She had already managed to get more syrup outside herself than in. Her dark matted hair had become stiff in places where she had brushed it from her face with syrupy hands.

"Mrs Pick," said Mum.

"Pick Nick!" boomed Boomer from his throne. "Pick Nick!"

"Who's she?" I asked, feeling rather worried. I hate having different people to sit for us. I like to know where I stand.

"She's one of my babysitting circle," said Mum. "She runs that pet beauty clinic in the High Street."

"Not that one where they clip the poodles and dye them pink?" I asked.

"Oh dear!" Mum said. "I seem to remember she's very neat and tidy."

She surveyed the untidy room as the door opened and Dad led in a tall, thin woman in a smart green dress.

"Good evening, everyone," said Mrs Pick. She turned to Mum. "You'd better introduce me to them all."

"This is Gus," said Mum. "Short for dis*gus*ting!"

"And An*gus*," I muttered.

Mrs Pick frowned at my chemistry set.

"And Yeti," said Mum. "Yeti has always had such an amazing shock of hair."

Mrs Pick's expression changed to dismay at the dripping syrup sandwich in Yeti's hand. Yeti grinned stickily.

"And Boomer," said Mum. "Well, you've only got to hear him ..."

Mrs Pick went pale, seeing what Boomer was sitting on.

"We're going to the Fire Station," said Dad. "It's a display on safety in the home."

"The children will show you where everything is," said Mum. "We'll only be gone a couple of hours."

"Try not to blow the house up, Gus!" said Dad, as he closed the door behind them.

Chapter 2
Sticky Everything

I began to get into my experiment. It was one I had never done before so I was trying to concentrate, but I didn't stand a chance.

"Er ... er ... Yeti?" I heard Mrs Pick say. "Er ... don't you think you've had enough syrup sandwiches for one day?"

"No," said Yeti. "Mum and Dad always let me have as many as I like."

I knew this was a downright, dirty lie, but I couldn't be bothered. I watched Yeti spreading her next slice and noticed the trickle of sticky golden liquid ooze over the edge of the table.

Punk, our cat, was right underneath. Round globules of syrup were landing in his black fur. He started licking. Boomer had noticed, too. He pointed at Punk.

"Licky Sticky," he boomed. "Licky Sticky!"

Punk spread the syrup with his tongue. It went right along his back. Then he rolled over on the pink patterned carpet. When he walked across the room a few moments later he had a line of pink wool down his backbone.

"Pinky Punky!" boomed Boomer, trying to grab Punk's tail. "Pinky Punky!"

He shuffled across the floor.

"Isn't it about time you got off that potty?" said Mrs Pick. "Have you finished?"

"Boomer finished!" boomed Boomer. "Boomer finished!"

"And it must be time for bed," said Mrs Pick.

"No bed!" boomed Boomer. "No bed!"

"Come on now ... er ... er ... Boomer," said Mrs Pick and she tried to lift Boomer off the potty.

But Boomer was stuck.

"Botty in potty!" boomed Boomer. "Botty in potty!"

Yeti giggled. I tried to concentrate on my experiment.

"Er ... Gus," said Mrs Pick. "Help me, will you?"

I sighed and stood up. My experiment would have to wait. I hung on to the potty while Mrs Pick pulled Boomer.

"Ready, steady, heave!" said Mrs Pick.

We heaved and tugged for ages. I had begun to think Boomer would have to stay stuck on the potty for ever! Then there was a sound like a cork coming out of a bottle.

I landed on the floor, clutching the potty. Luckily, it was empty! Mrs Pick flew backwards with Boomer in her arms. She landed flat on her back across the syrupy table.

"Ugh!" she said, pulling herself up and plonking Boomer on the floor. "Just look at me."

Bits of runny sandwich were clinging to her back as buttery syrup slid down her smart, green dress and on to the floor.

"My dress! Look at it! It's ruined!" she cried. "Now what am I going to do?"

"Wash it," I said. "You could wear Mum's dressing gown while it's in the wash. It's upstairs in Mum and Dad's room."

Mrs Pick disappeared upstairs. I sat down at the table and tried to remember where I had got to in my experiment. How can a bloke expect to split the atom when people interrupt him all the time?

After a few minutes, Mrs Pick reappeared wearing Mum's frilly nightie.

I sniggered. Yeti's eyes nearly popped out of her head. Boomer stood up and pointed his fat finger.

"Silly frilly!" he boomed. "Silly frilly!"

"This is all I could find," Mrs Pick snapped. "Now where's that washing machine?"

I took her to the kitchen. I tried to tell her about the washing machine having a mind of its own, but she wouldn't listen. She shoved the dress in with some soap powder and switched on. We went back into the dining-room. A puddle had appeared on the floor at Boomer's feet.

"Good boy, Boomer!" he boomed. "Good boy, Boomer!"

"No. Bad boy, Boomer!" said Mrs Pick. "Where's the mop?"

When I had shown her where the mop and bucket were kept, I went back to my experiment. I felt really cheesed off. I bet that boffin Einstein never had this trouble!

At that moment, the front door bell rang.

Chapter 3
Woof and Mr Barker

Mrs Pick froze.

"Who's that?" she asked.

I shrugged my shoulders. How could I tell? I haven't got X-Ray eyes, have I?

Mrs Pick began to panic.

"I can't have anyone seeing me like this," she said. She dropped the mop and flung herself over the back of the settee.

I went to the front door.

"Hey!" I said, seeing my best mate, Woof, and his Dad, Mr Barker, on the step. (Woof's only his nickname, by the way.) "Come in."

They followed me inside. Mr Barker looked at Yeti with her syrup sandwiches and Boomer with the puddle on the floor. Then he looked at my experiment on the table.

"I've come to arrange Saturday's football practice," he said. "Are your Mum and Dad in?"

I shook my head.

"We've got a babysitter," I said.

"Oh," said Mr Barker. "Where?"

I shifted from one foot to the other. I didn't want to lie to him, but I couldn't really tell the truth, could I?

"Well," I said. "She's around here somewhere. Only she's not available at the moment."

"Oh," said Mr Barker.

We agreed on a time for the football and I promised to tell Dad.

"Are you sure everything's all right?" asked Mr Barker as I let him and Woof out of the front door.

"Sure," I said.

Back in the dining-room, Mrs Pick popped up from behind the settee. Her hair looked like a blackbird's nest, full of dust, sweet papers and last week's bread crusts.

"I'd better put ... er ... Boomer to bed," she said, but Boomer had other ideas. He dived under the table.

"Come out from there at once," said Mrs Pick, but Boomer refused to budge.

"Er ... Gus, will you help me?" Mrs Pick said. "Tell ... er ... Boomer, it's time to go to bed."

But this time I was busy adding the next ingredient to my experiment. I pretended I hadn't heard her. Mrs Pick sighed and turned to Yeti.

"Now ... er ... Yeti," she said. "It's time to clear away your mess."

"I haven't finished," said Yeti. "Mum said I could eat the whole tin of syrup if I wanted."

Mrs Pick opened her mouth to reply when the doorbell rang again.

Chapter 4
A Revolting Smell

"Oh no," said Mrs Pick. "I wonder who it can be this time."

She shot under the table with Boomer. I went straight to the door. It was Mr Brass, my trumpet teacher. I invited him in.

"I'm afraid I've got to cancel your lesson this week," he said.

"That's a pity," I said. I enjoy my trumpet playing. It's great to see everyone deafened for half an hour each day!

Mr Brass was looking round at the dreadful mess.

"Are your parents in?" he asked.

I repeated the bit about the babysitter being around somewhere. I promised to pass on the message about the trumpet lesson and got rid of Mr Brass as soon as I could. He gave me a funny look as I closed the door.

This time, Mrs Pick emerged looking like she had come in from a force ten storm.

"Oh dear," she said. "I wonder how much longer your parents are going to be."

I added another ingredient to my experiment. It was beginning to look interesting. It was a putrid shade of green with small purple bubbles slowly rising to the surface. I felt pleased with myself. This experiment was turning out well. I watched it bubbling away. It reminded me of Mum's cooking! I suddenly felt very hungry.

"I usually have my supper about now," I said.

"Oh dear," she said again. "What do you usually have?"

"I fancy some fish fingers," I said. "Please," I added, remembering my manners for once.

I don't usually have fish fingers, but if my sister was getting away with eating a whole tin of syrup, why shouldn't I have something I fancy, too?

Mrs Pick scowled at me, but after a moment she got up and went to the kitchen. I heard her

delving into the freezer and rattling the grill pan.

A revolting smell rose from my experiment. It nearly knocked me off my chair. Yeti stuffed her syrup sandwiches into her mouth to protect them from the stench. Boomer poked his head out from under the table and held his nose.

"Stinky stink!" he said. "Stinky stink!"

By the time Mrs Pick came back, I had gone off the idea of fish fingers. She nearly passed out with the smell. She staggered to the window and flung it open. Then she found a spray can and waved it all over the room. I couldn't decide which smell was worse – my experiment or the spray.

The washing machine's final spin began to rock the house. I hung on to Mum's best vase as it wobbled across the table. The roaring died down and the washing machine stopped

spinning. Mrs Pick went to fetch her dress from the kitchen. After a few minutes, she rushed back into the room with the dress in her hands.

"Look!" she yelled, holding it up against her. "It's shrunk! I'll never get into that!"

I had tried to warn her! It wouldn't have fitted Boomer, let alone Mrs Pick!

I couldn't believe it when the door bell rang for the third time.

Chapter 5
The Police Investigate

As soon as I spotted the two police-officers on the door step, my brain went into overdrive. I thought that Mum and Dad must have had an accident. They were lying in hospital. They were dead and we were orphans. Mrs Pick was the serial child killer they had been hunting for. She poisoned her victims with fish fingers and syrup. The police-officer showed me his ID.

"And you are ...?" he asked.

"Gus," I said.

"Can we come in?" asked the policewoman.

"I don't see why not," I said, still wondering why they had come. I backed along the hallway, hoping they wouldn't notice the smell, but the policewoman held her nose.

"What's going on, Gus?" she asked.

"Nothing much," I said.

I led them into the dining-room. Yeti was still at the table, almost totally coated in golden syrup. Boomer was hugging Punk and they were licking each other to clean off the syrup. There was no sign of Mrs Pick.

"I thought as much," said the policeman. "We've had two reports this evening, from Mr Barker and Mr Brass."

I sighed with relief. Our parents were all right. Mrs Pick was not a serial killer.

"Parents gone out, have they?" asked the policeman.

"Yes," I said. What had Mr Barker and Mr Brass been saying?

"Left you on your own, have they?" asked the policewoman. "Tut, tut."

"Tut, tut, tutty, tutty!" boomed Boomer. "Tut, tut, tutty, tutty!"

"You've got it all wrong," I said. "We've got a babysitter."

"Are you expecting us to believe that?" asked the policeman. "There's no babysitter here."

"There is!" I said. "Honest. She's called Mrs Pick."

"Pick nose!" boomed Boomer, showing how far his finger would go. "Pick nose!"

"Mrs Pick!" shouted the policeman, trying to ignore Boomer. "Come on out wherever you are."

Mrs Pick, looking like the Wild Woman from the West, stepped out from behind the curtains.

"What's going on?" asked the policewoman again.

"It's quite simple, really," said Mrs Pick.

I let the two officers out of the front door a few minutes later, after Mrs Pick had tried to explain everything. When I got back into the dining-room, the smell of burning took over from the stench of my experiment and the pong of the spray.

Suddenly, the shrill squeal of the smoke alarm deafened us all. Black smoke began to seep under the kitchen door.

"Oh, no!" I yelled. "We've forgotten the fish fingers!"

Mrs Pick rushed into the kitchen. She dashed through the smoke, coughing and spluttering. She threw the grill pan and the burning fish fingers out into the back yard.

"Open the front door," she yelled, as she collapsed onto the settee. "Let the smoke out."

I didn't need a second telling! Smoke billowed around me as I pulled open the door.

"How do you turn off that alarm?" she shouted when I got back.

I shrugged my shoulders.

"I don't know," I shouted.

"I wish Mum and Dad were here," Yeti shouted as she clapped her syrupy hands over her ears.

Chapter 6
Parents up the Pole

While all this was going on at home, Mum and Dad were enjoying their evening out. They had listened to a talk by the Fire Chief on accidents in the home. They had seen films of burning houses and daring rescues.

"Now," said the Fire Chief. "It's time for you to find out how fit we have to be for this job."

Mum tried on some breathing apparatus and rescued a dummy from a smoke-filled room. Dad learned how to put out a burning pan of cooking oil. They both had a go at sliding down the firemen's pole.

Ten minutes later, Mum was right at the top of the turntable ladder and was about to climb through a window. Dad was fighting with a snaking hose with the water turned full on. At that moment, the Chief's bleep started flashing.

"Sorry, folks!" he shouted. "We've got a call."

"Oh dear," said Mum. "Someone's house on fire? How terrible!"

She managed to climb down the ladder. Dad turned off the water and gained control of the hose.

A few seconds later, the fire engine rocketed out of the double doors of the Fire Station and sped along the road.

Chapter 7
Everything Bubbles Over

I couldn't stand the high pitched squeal of the alarm a second longer, so I shut the kitchen door. I thought that might dull the sound. But somehow the squealing seemed to be getting louder, even though my hands were pressed firmly over my ears. Then the light from the hall began flashing white then blue, white, blue, blue, blue, blue ...

"Where's the fire?" yelled a voice, making me jump and knock over my test tube.

I watched in horror as my experiment spread rapidly and bubbled over the edge of the table. You'll never guess who was underneath – Punk!

That was when the Fire Chief burst in, hose in hand! He narrowly missed trampling on Boomer, stepped in the potty, tripped over the mop and landed with his head in Mrs Pick's lap!

"We've had a 999 call," he yelled as he got up. "Where's the fire?"

Then he sniffed and turned up his nose.

"That's disgusting! What on earth is it?"

"It's Punk," I shouted.

"More like Skunk!" yelled the Chief.

"Punk Skunk!" boomed Boomer. "Punk Skunk!"

Three more fire fighters ran in. The first was carrying a fire blanket. The second was unwinding a hose. The third was waving an axe above his head. They stopped dead in their tracks and held their noses.

"How did you get here so fast?" I yelled. "We haven't even called you yet."

Suddenly, the smoke alarm went silent. We all looked at each other. I was tensed up, waiting for it to start again, but it didn't. The kitchen door opened and Mrs Chatter from next door came in.

"I've turned that dreadful noise off," she said, as if we hadn't noticed. "I heard it going from inside my house so I opened my door to see where it came from. I could smell burning. When I saw such thick, black smoke pouring out of your doors and windows, I called the Fire Brigade."

Mrs Chatter got out a tissue and covered her nose. She looked from Mrs Pick to Yeti and her syrup, to Boomer and his puddle, then to me and my evil-smelling test tube.

"Gus," she said, "what's going on?"

"I think I'll put the cat out," I said.

I carried Punk the Skunk into the garden, then chucked what was left of my experiment into the dustbin. I didn't like doing that. What a waste of a good stink! That might have come in handy in the future!

When I got back indoors, the police-officers had returned. They were making notes. Mr Brass and Mr Barker and Woof had come back too, to check that we were all right. They all sat round the room listening to Mrs Pick. She was trying to explain everything to everyone. Boomer was trying to help.

"Stinky stinky!" he boomed. "Skunky Punky! Good boy, Boomer!"

Then I noticed Yeti. She had been very quiet and I had almost forgotten about her in the excitement. The syrup tin was empty! I couldn't make out how she had eaten all that syrup without being violently sick. Still, there was plenty of time for that. In fact, she was already looking a delicate shade of green!

"Anyone for a cup of tea?" I asked.

Then, as if the house wasn't full enough already, two more fire fighters burst in. They stood and stared at all the people. Then they took off their helmets. I had the surprise of my life! It was Mum and Dad!

"What's going on, Gus?" asked Mum.

"And what's that disgusting smell?" asked Dad.

Chapter 8
A Perfect Pong

Suddenly, Mrs Pick threw back her head and roared with laughter. Then she jumped up onto a chair in the middle of the room. Everyone turned to stare at her.

"This has been such a wild and wonderful evening!" she announced to our amazement.

I gripped the table to stop myself falling off my chair with the shock. Then I wished I hadn't. My hands were coated in the remains of Yeti's syrup.

"Yuk!" I said, but Mrs Pick hadn't finished.

"I've had the most exciting and crazy time of my life!" she said.

I could see Mum and Dad were nearly as knocked over as I was by what she was saying.

"You have three lovely children," Mrs Pick said to them. "Boomer's absolutely super!"

Boomer stopped licking the carpet for a moment and sat up.

"Super dooper Boomer!" he boomed. "Super dooper Boomer!"

A smile lit up Mrs Pick's face.

"And Yeti's a darling," said Mrs Pick.

Yeti tried to smile, but her face was stiff with the layer of syrup that still covered it.

"As for Gus," said Mrs Pick, "he'll soon be Young Scientist of the Year!"

I gulped. She was being sarcastic. Either that or she had flipped, fallen out of her tree, got a few screws loose!

But the smile on Mrs Pick's face made her look really different. Almost like a human being! Perhaps she really *had* enjoyed herself after all?

Then, Punk walked in.

"Look out!" I yelled.

"Stinky Skunky Punky!" boomed Boomer. "Stinky Skunky Punky!"

I dived at the cat, ready to throw him out again. *Nobody* would be able to stand that stench any more.

But I had forgotten the mop which still lay where Mrs Pick had dropped it.

I tripped and landed with my nose right in Punk's fur which was wet from the rain outside. I pushed myself away, expecting the foul smell to fill my nostrils. But I was wrong.

What's going on, Gus? I asked myself.

A sweet scent rose from the cat's wet fur. I saw Mrs Pick sniff. Her eyes lit up as she took a flying leap off the chair and pounced on the cat.

"Perfect!" she said. She thrust Punk into my arms and dashed from the room. Nobody moved or made a sound. After a few minutes, Mrs Pick rushed back in, holding my test tube at arm's length. I watched her go to the sink and add a few drops of water to the test tube.

"A perfect pong!" cried Mrs Pick, as the smell changed.

"Perfect Pong!" boomed Boomer. "Perfect Pong!"

"Hooray!" cried Mrs Pick. "Well done, Gus!"

"What have I done now?" I asked.

"I've been searching for this for a long time," said Mrs Pick. "And now you've invented it. A perfume for posh pets."

"You can't be serious!" I said.

"This will make you a fortune!" said Mrs Pick. "The perfect pong for the millennium. But what can we call it?"

"Posh Pet Perfume!" boomed Boomer. "Posh Pet Perfume!"

"Good boy, Boomer," I said. Then I laughed.

It hadn't been such a bad evening, after all!

Other Barrington Stoke titles available:-

Hostage by Malorie Blackman 1-902260-12-0

Ghost for Sale by Terry Deary 1-902260-14-7

Billy the Squid by Colin Dowland 1-902260-04-X

Kick Back by Vivian French 1-902260-02-3

The Gingerbread House by Adèle Geras 1-902260-03-1

Virtual Friend by Mary Hoffman 1-902260-00-7

Tod in Biker City by Anthony Masters 1-902260-15-5

Wartman by Michael Morpurgo 1-902260-05-8

Extra Time by Jenny Oldfield 1-902260-13-9

Screw Loose by Alison Prince 1-902260-01-5

Lift Off by Hazel Townson 1-902260-11-2

If you would like more information about the **BARRINGTON STOKE CLUB**, please write to:- Barrington Stoke Club, 10 Belford Terrace, Edinburgh, EH4 3DQ or visit our website at:- www.barringtonstoke.co.uk